MARSHALL CAVENDISH CLASSICS

THE NEW ARMY DAZE

The New Army Daze

MICHAEL CHIANG

First published in 1985 by Times Editions

This edition published in 2021 by Marshall Cavendish Editions
An imprint of Marshall Cavendish International

Other Marshall Cavendish Offices:
Marshall Cavendish Corporation, 800 Westchester Ave, Suite N-641, Rye Brook, NY 10573, USA • Marshall Cavendish International (Thailand) Co Ltd, 253 Asoke, 16th Floor, Sukhumvit 21 Road, Klongtoey Nua, Wattana, Bangkok 10110, Thailand • Marshall Cavendish (Malaysia) Sdn Bhd, Times Subang, Lot 46, Subang Hi-Tech Industrial Park, Batu Tiga, 40000 Shah Alam, Selangor Darul Ehsan, Malaysia

National Library Board, Singapore Cataloguing in Publication Data

Name(s): Chiang, Michael.
Title: The new army daze / Michael Chiang.
Other title(s): Marshall Cavendish classics.
Description: Singapore : Marshall Cavendish Editions, 2021. | First published in 1985 by Times Editions.
Identifier(s): OCN 1253292811 | ISBN 978-981-4974-52-3 (paperback)
Subject(s): LCSH: National service--Singapore--Humor. | National service--Singapore--Anecdotes. | Singapore--Armed Forces--Military life--Humor. | Singapore--Armed Forces--Military life--Anecdotes.
Classification: DDC 355.10922--dc23

Illustrations by CHEAH

Printed in Singapore

Contents

Introduction 7
Separating the Men from the Boys 9
Tumbling In 14
Morning Has Broken – Go Clean Up The Mess 19
I Married an M-16 23
Eating In or Take Away? 27
How To Speak Genitalia 32
Let's Get Physical 50
Please Don't Rain On My Parade 57
Welcome to the Pressure Dome 62
Everything But the Girls 67
Enemy in Front, Charge! 71
A-Camping We Will Go 75
Halt! Who Goes There? 82
Should I Sign On? 88
Relax, Don't Do It 94
And So It Came to Pass 98
I'm Recalling You-oo-oo-oo! 102

Introduction

Some men are born to be soldiers.

Many, many others are not.

So, for generations, less heroically-inclined males could afford to twiddle their thumbs and other appendages while the robust hunks charged to the front line and made careers out of the army.

Then came National Service.

And like a bolt from the blue beyond, it shot into the home of the Everyman, and forever changed the quiet, mundane lives of us non-macho types.

There were those who took it bravely, of course. They started to read war comics, began to acquire a penchant for articles of green clothing, and developed a yen for PE lessons.

The majority preferred to resort to hysteria and other well-known forms of desperate panic-to no avail.

When National Service was first initiated in 1968, the army didn't quite know how tough to come down on its new batch of reluctant soldiers, who were themselves convinced that they were getting the worst end of the bargain.

But time soothes many ills.

And so it came to pass that National Service became firmly ensconced in the social fabric of life, an accepted fact of growing up male in Singapore.

Today, the army is no longer a rude four-letter word. It is many other things. An initiation into manhood, a stepping-stone to success, a springboard into adult society.

Oftentimes, it is also a pain in the posterior.

Separating the Men from the Boys

I wish I had played soldiers in my childhood.

But no, I had to choose to be part of that elite corps of seven-year-olds who frittered away precious weekends playing doctor. In white smocks (father's shirts), surgical masks (mother's sanitary napkins), and plastic stethoscopes, we struck terror into the hearts of little kindergarten girls in the neighbourhood.

None of us foresaw that 10 years later we would be forced to play soldiers. And that we wouldn't be using toy guns or plastic grenades either.

Thus it was that I approached my 18th birthday with some trepidation. By then, I had heard all about National Service or NS. Much of the news hadn't been good.

After attempts to alter the sex on my birth certificate had failed, I decided to put up a false front and accept my calling gracefully.

The year before enlistment, I duly turned up for my registration at the CMPB (Central Manpower

Base) armed with documents and an air of gallant resignation.

As I sat in the large room waiting to be processed for the army records, I surveyed the rest of my luckless generation. All aged 17 or thereabouts, they were generally bespectacled and ashen-faced. Like me.

It was tense. Now and then, someone would cough self-consciously. Always one to face adversity with a cool, unruffled mind, I oozed nonchalance and took out my knitting needles to begin work on my 100 per cent lamb's wool vest. Green, of course.

Eyes, no doubt burning with awe and admiration, gazed intently at me as my needles stabbed a silent code into the air.

It wasn't long before I was called forward to present my papers. I gave them a copy of *The Straits Times.* But they'd already read it and asked for my birth certificate and school certs instead. I obliged.

Then I was shunted down a corridor into another room where I realised that there would be no turning back. I was headed for that dreaded medical check-up which would seal my fate forever. My legs tried to take on the semblance of jelly and succeeded.

"Take off your clothes and line up behind that door," droned a bored little clerk.

I blistered with indignation at his audacity, but obeyed. Not least because he was flanked by two

BLAM

BLAM
BLAM
BLAM
BLAM
BLAM
BLAM

oversized medical orderlies who looked like their main purpose in life was to beat dissidents into unrecognisable pulp.

As I stood there in my Giordano briefs trying to salvage what little was left of my modesty with strategic positioning of the elbows, I pondered my sorry existence. Surely this moment would go down in history as one of the low points of my life.

The medical examination began with the customary measurement of weight and height. Then a nurse of sorts stapled my index finger to the table as some blood was removed for testing. No one heeded my screams.

I was then moved into another room where there sat a musty-faced doctor who scowled like a failed gynaecologist bent on vengeance.

"Pull down your briefs," he barked, "and cough!"

At the sight of the scalpel lying on his desk, I lost control of my throat muscles. I let out a whine.

It threw the doctor into momentary confusion. He quickly regained his composure and made a sudden lunge for my jugular. I coughed so hard my tonsils nearly shot out.

My recollections of the rest of the medical test are, as you may well imagine, somewhat hazy, diminished in significance by that encounter with the mad doctor. What is significant is the fact that I passed the test. I was certified combat-fit.

The news severely impaired my sense of humour. I no longer enjoyed watching *Tour of Duty.*

Tumbling In

Like most misguided youths, I believed one could actually psyche oneself into liking the army.

I began by buying two volumes of *Famous Marches of the World* by Mantovani and his *Music of the Mountains,* in the hope that I might discover the aesthetic qualities of an army parade. The records cured my mother's insomnia but did nothing for me.

After consulting friends, I came to the conclusion that physique could make or break one's soldiering fortune. I bought a pair of Asics running shoes and made impressive notations on my calendar indicating a rigorous timetable of thrice-weekly runs.

I ran around the car park twice the first day.

I never went on the second and third runs that week.

I was discharged from hospital only 10 days later.

It seemed easier to practise push-ups in the privacy of my bedroom. I managed four at my first attempt but also sprained my back and left wrist. Things didn't seem to be going too well.

So I discarded my get-fit campaign and decided to train my stomach for the notorious army food-despite having prayed that the unsavoury rumours about army food weren't true. Several self-cooked meals later, I was flat out in defeat. They kept the same bed in the same ward for me.

I figured that there was some sublime message in all this and threw all caution to the monsoon. I decided to live a totally debauched life right till I was conscripted. Two and a half years was long enough, why suffer prematurely?

The day came sooner than anticipated. Lugging my overnight bag bulging with Kit Kat, Yeo's packet drinks, Kleenex, new underwear, mosquito coils, Lux, Colgate, plastic bags and other survival items, I returned to the CMPB. The place had a whiff of familiarity, the kind one can happily live without.

But strangely enough, the mood was anything but tense. It was, believe it or not, festive. Mothers, girlfriends, and an assortment of relatives cackled with well-meaning advice.

"Make sure you point rifle the other way, ah, boy," nagged one mother.

"Don't share toothbrush, okay?" snapped another.

Some mothers blinked back a tear or two, some grinned malevolently, some yawned.

Mine pushed me out of the car and drove off laughing.

The sons mostly looked spaced-out, smiling like TV game-show contestants waiting for a booby prize.

The men in the green uniforms seemed happiest. They fawned over their new wards, exchanged pleasantries with the boys' relatives, made goo-goo conversation with toddlers and beamed at all and sundry until their cheeks ached. Never had I seen SAF soldiers so friendly.

As we were herded onto our respective three-tonners amid the final goodbyes, the SAF men were still joking with us.

As the vehicles drove out of the CMPB, I felt encouraged to try to make conversation with the sergeant in charge.

I was dicing with death. It took four men to prevent the friendly sergeant from biting my right ear off. It was a crucial lesson in human behaviour. It dawned on me how low a life form recruits were.

The three-tonners eventually reached our designated camp, at about the same time that all of us had been reduced to a suitable level of despondency.

Wrought with gross feelings of inadequacy, we moved about our immediate tasks with utmost servility. We accepted our oversized uniforms with expressions of profound gratitude, wept tears of joy at the sight of

our wonderful living quarters, and allowed ourselves to be overwhelmed by a sense of divine privilege when told to scrub the floor.

We feigned ecstasy when summoned for our tropical haircuts, but nonetheless stole a quick look in the mirror at the last vestiges of our adolescence.

If Hitler had been reincarnated, I'm sure he would have come back as an SAF barber.

"What style you want?" asked one barber genially.

I scanned the pictures on his wall and pointed to George Michael.

"Okay," he nodded.

Two minutes later, I was out of the chair, the back of my head looking like Sinead O'Connor. I made an intrepid attempt to maintain my composure.

We all looked alike. Puny bespectacled beings with heads like toilet brushes. No matter where I turned, I saw reflections of myself. It was most depressing.

I contemplated suicide that first night, but seeing how we had to get up early the next morning, I decided to sleep instead.

Morning Has Broken – Go Clean Up The Mess

One of the most precious things in the army is sleep. It is scarce, and it is in shortest supply when you are a trainee soldier and need it most.

As raw recruits, we were woken up by merciless NCOs at 4:30 a.m. I jest you not. 4:30 a.m. The time at which my brain cells are at their most restful state. Peaceful. Comatose.

But fresh young soldiers are not meant to waste their time between the sheets.

"Wake up! Wake up! Faibee axe! Faibee axe!" hollered the duty corporal.

By some supernatural strength, we dragged our bodies down to the parade square. The moon was still high.

We proceeded with 5 BX, the army's basic exercises guaranteed to put fire into your soul and bounce into your body at 5 in the morning. We stretched our limbs in between yawns, did star-jumps as our eyelids tried to defy the laws of gravity, and sought to wobble our bodies to life.

The hardest were the sit-ups. Half the men fell asleep the instant their heads touched ground. Exercises at horizontal position should not be encouraged in 5 BX.

The sessions usually ended with a brisk run around the camp area. It never failed to completely nullify what little zest the earlier exercises had instilled.

After a quick breakfast that saw us wolfing down eggs neither hard- nor half-boiled, bread that had as much flavour as bleached diapers, and tea that tasted like Colombian coffee, we set out to wage our daily war.

The infamous SAF War Against Dirt. An all-consuming army passion innocuously called "area-cleaning."

Pampered young sons who had no previous knowledge of housework faced a rude awakening. The more awkward one looked with a broom and brush, the more likely one would be despatched to clean the toilets.

I learnt fast. By the second day, I acted as if I could engage the mop in intimate tete-a-tete. They were highly impressed and made me full-time toilet cleaner.

There was no end to what needed to be cleaned in the army camps. The parade square had to be swept clear of leaves every morning. The drains had to be swept clear of leaves every morning. The roads had to be swept clear of leaves every morning. Those blasted leaves, I swear, were deliberately scattered by human hands while we slept.

The offices required their share of sweeping, dusting and mopping. Yet also without fail, the dust and dirt reappeared in all the same places in the midst of night. My theory is that the ceiling fan is a deviously-conceived contraption which sucks in dirt through the windows in the day and redistributes it all over the office when dusk falls.

The toilet bowls were my chief source of misery. I couldn't understand why cleaning them was such a cheerful and jubilant pastime on television.

Anyway, most of the bacteria were under control by 7 a.m., when we prepared to face another line of fire. In the name of good hygiene, the SAF organised another infamy: the stand-by-bed. Uniforms frantically ironed the night before would be inspected, as would be boots, mess tins, and all other personal items displayed in the lockers.

My platoon commander was a hard man to please.

"Recruit," he hissed into my nostrils, "what is this eyelash doing on your bar of soap? Drop 10!"

The first time I didn't know what he meant and started to pluck out the said number of eyelashes. Realising it wasn't what he wanted, I thought I'd try collapsing heavily onto the floor several times.

Looking back, I realised how ridiculous I must

have looked. No one stopped me at that time because they figured I was having an unusual form of epileptic seizure.

Such was the manner in which I passed many memorable mornings in the army. Mornings when I missed sleep more than anything else in the world.

Except maybe a Filipina maid.

I Married an M-16

At first it sounded like a practical joke.

"As a soldier, you must treat your rifle like your wife," said the sergeant. We recruits tittered sardonically.

Then we heard talk about marriage, and wondered about the "handing-over ceremony" scheduled to take place that night. We knew there and then that these guys weren't joking.

The thought was odious. Here I was, barely out of my pimply teens, poised to savour the bubbly wine of youth. And there they were, planning to foist marriage upon me.

I insisted on a compatibility test. The armskote man spat in my face.

I tried to negotiate for a reasonable dowry to offset the severe emotional trauma I was going through. I was curtly told that the in-laws could not be contacted.

The hours ticked by without mercy. My heart bled for the relatives who had pampered me in my pubescent years in the hope that I might one day marry one of

BLAM! BLAM! BLAM! BLAM!

their daughters and throw an elaborate 10-course dinner at Shang Palace.

What pained me more was that there would be no wedding cake. There would also be no wedding gifts.

I was besieged by troubling visions of microwave ovens, crock pots and bed-linen vanishing into thin air. When I came to, the ceremony was about to begin.

In retrospect, I must admit that a romantic aura did fill the humid air that sultry night. There, around the open square, where my bachelor hood would be terminated in one fell swoop, were rows and rows of little lamps that bathed the soldiers in a surreal, magical glow.

I chose to ignore the fact that the jahudi lamps were nothing more than condensed milk tins filled with sand and kerosene and lit with a dirty old wick.

The darkened splendour of that tropical night so moved me that I decided to resist my fate no longer. I would yield my tender body to the raptures of marriage. The fact that I was threatened with another haircut if I didn't go through with the ceremony may have had a slight bearing on my decision.

So there we were, lambs for the sacrifice.

There was no music, only the strange wheezing sound from one of the asthmatic soldiers.

I strode purposefully to the altar where my intended lay. There, clad in a thin layer of oil, reclined my M-16. She glistened seductively in the eerie light.

I brushed aside my prejudices against arranged marriages and the vows were recited. Then I stretched out my virginal hands and took her gently into my arms and marched solemnly back to my platoon. It was an emotional experience.

Later that evening, in the privacy of our quarters, I stripped her and explored her, poring over her every feature.

Her bolt-carrier. Her safety pin. Her barrel. Her foresight tip. Her zeroing mechanism. Her trigger. She had untold mysteries awaiting my discovery.

Ours was not love at first sight, but an affection born of time and experience. Before long, I knew all there was to know about her. I could relate to her. And when we finally consummated our relationship on the firing range, it was loud and passionate.

In the aftermath, when we returned exhausted to my barracks, I realised that the ways of love were indeed strange. Inexplicably, I had fallen madly in love with my own M-16.

There was nothing more I yearned for.

Except a pleasant way of telling my parents that their daughter-in-law could not cook.

Eating In or Take Away?

The one aspect of army life that arouses the most interest is army food.

"Why, it was almost as bad as army food!" Laugh, laugh, laugh.

"Oh come on, nothing can be as bad as army food!" Guffaw, guffaw. Nudge, nudge.

Such jokes demean the army cook's vocation. And it was these unpleasant insinuations that caused my cousin, a cook trained during his NS, to retire to a monastery in Ipoh where he is living on raw vegetables and pomelo for the rest of his life.

I wish people would be more aware of the sensitivities involved before making army cooking the butt of their rude wisecracks. Wisecracks that are not only tasteless but stale. Just like the army food in some camps.

The army believes in complete training and it is often true that by the end of NS, a soldier's toughest muscles are those located in his stomach. This is extremely useful in times of war, when troops may be required to withstand great stress and consume challenging food.

It is towards preparing the soldier for such states of emergency that the army takes utmost care in its kitchens.

Only tough, sinewy beef is good enough for the men. Nothing invigorates stomach muscles like a piece of beef textured like Goodyear tyres.

Bland, fat chickens are prized. As is fatty pork. These flabby meats make any kind of seasoning taste good.

Vegetables always arrive at the camps fresh, green and healthy. These attributes are not in keeping with war-torn conditions, which army cooks try at all times to simulate.

Vegetables that get fresh are usually treated with much contempt and left to do penance in musty closets overnight. The next day, deviant plants show visible signs of remorse. Whereupon they are thrown into the pan and severely overcooked.

Sweet and sour pork and curry beef are staples on most cookhouse menus. After a few months, an NS man learns to distinguish between the two.

It is often said that the army serves its troops rice salvaged from World War II. This is a vicious rumour. The rice actually comes from Kelantan's bumper harvest of 1966.

FISH
BEEF
CHICKEN
MUTTON

Tea and coffee are served during breakfast and sometimes after night training. Some soldiers have been known to take the liquid home by the bottles for a variety of purposes. It can be used to stain woodwork, fertilise gardens, lubricate Daihatsu Charade engines and cure breast cancer.

It is rumoured that an application by an NS man to patent and market the stuff was rejected by MINDEF in 1979.

At the slightest chance, soldiers dash out to the canteen for their supplementary diet. As the canteen is out of bounds most hours of the day, soldiers are generally forced to stock their own food in the barracks.

By and large, instant noodles are the most popular. With the aid of a heating coil-a device which manages somehow to resemble both an egg-beater and a mosquito coil-water is boiled in a huge enamel mug. This is used to cook the noodles, which are then drained and eaten with chilli sauce. The connoisseurs add a dash of sesame oil and garnish with mother's own fried shallots. Only the plebeians use Cerebos Chicken Floss.

Between meals, soldiers snack on biscuits and drink Yeo's packet drinks, usually sugarcane. The stuff is green and blends easily with the uniform if spilled.

Most NS men put on weight during their stints in

the army. Mothers tell their friends that the army feeds their sons well.

Blessed are the ignorant.

How To Speak Genitalia

A favourite pastime in the army is talking cock.

This has no sexual overtones. It merely involves getting together after training or during breaks to talk rubbish.

The expression can also be used as an admonishment. "Don't talk cock!" is an appropriate response to a trainee's suggestion that guard duty be extended to officers.

To get by in the SAF, it hence becomes necessary to develop one's skill at talking cock. The more nonsense you spout, the more likely you are going to be welcome in any soldiering fraternity.

The army has its own favourite phrases and expressions, and it is imperative that new soldiers pick up these verbal delights as soon as possible. While some believe that the ability to swear in at least three dialects is sufficient to see you through your NS, many other schools of thought are more inclined to feel that army slanging is the way to win friends and influence people.

A person of average intelligence should be able to function normally as an NS man with the following glossary:

Ar

(Hokkien) Favour, as in currying favour.
Example: "This officer can ar one, man."
(Translated: This officer is one with whom one can negotiate.)

Ar ka liau

(Hokkien) One who is totally ar-gable.

Ar ka chi

(Hokkien) Ditto.

Aqua (ar kwa)

(Hokkien) Not a mineral water, but an effeminate soldier. High propensity for melodrama during training.

Armskoteman

Duty person assigned to look after arms. (Legs tend to look after themselves.)

Attend B

Doctor's prescription. Means a soldier can only perform light duties-but cannot switch off.

Attend C

More valuable doctor's prescription. Equivalent to an MC-now he can switch off.

AWOL

Absent without leave. Offence that could get you castrated.

Balls drop

Not really related to the above. It means loss of nerve, fear.

Example: "Want to apply for day off, see Encik's face straightaway balls drop."

(Translated: I had intended to make an application for a day's leave, but lost my nerve when I caught sight of the Company Sergeant Major's stern demeanour.)

Bang balls

To be frustrated.

Basha

Those campy little tents army boys build out in the field.

Blank

Devoid of intelligence. (See "blur.")

Blank file

Used in drills. Describes the empty space between the ranks. Space where a soldier should be standing. Used as a description, refers to the missing tooth or teeth of a particular soldier.
Example: One Blank File can be used as a name for the guy with the missing front tooth.

Blanket party

Celebration where guests wear only bed coverings. Seriously folks, it refers to a ritual soldiers sometimes put unpopular members of their group through. Procedure: During lights-off, a blanket is thrown over the offending party, covering him completely. His mates then rain punches on him. (Caution: Avoid picking blanket with too many holes if you prefer to remain incognito.)

Blue Thunder

(See "helicopter")

Blur

Daft, dense, dumb. Also, blur like sotong.

Blur king

One who is the epitome of blur-ness.

Burnt

Gone, destroyed, up in smoke. Used to describe that weekend which has been assigned to you for guard duty.

Bozo

One who ought to join the circus; clown.

CB leaf

A broad leaf trainees are discouraged from using as camouflage during field training. Decency forbids the explanation of CB.

Chari point

(Malay) To look for marks; to try and score points. Describes those trying to get into the good books of superiors.

Chiak chuah

(Hokkien) Eat snake; play truant; to escape work and training.

Chiak he

(Hokkien) Eat fish. Used to describe a superior who is extremely strict. (See "ngeow.")

Chicken backside

What SAF barbers model the backs of soldiers' hairstyles after.

Chochok

(Malay) To instigate; to make trouble.

Climb on top

To take advantage.
Example: "Just because I am nice to you doesn't mean you can climb on top of me, okay!"

Cock-up

Oh scrub your filthy mind, it's nothing like that! Refers to the jamming of the rifle mechanism, but also used to describe a malfunction or problem encountered in everyday situations. A hopelessly inept soldier can, for example, cock-up his platoon's exercise.

Condemned

Those with no future in the army.

Crab

Crustacean popularly cooked with chilli sauce, available at seafood restaurants along East Coast Road and Pulau Tekong. Also, the crown worn by army majors on their epaulettes.

Debrief

What one wears under de pants. Also refers to the post-mortem conducted after a training exercise.

Double-up

To speed up; on the double.

Drop

Prefix to a number of push-ups. "Drop 20!" is an instruction to do 20 push-ups.

Dry run

Unsuccessful wet dream. Actually, a rehearsal for an important field exercise. Before a live firing exercise (for example, one using real ammunition), it is customary to conduct a dry run using blanks.

Elephants

The specks of dirt found in the barrel of a soldier's rifle during inspection.
Example: "Recruit Tan! You think this is the Mandai Zoo, is it?"
"No, sir!"
"So what are these bloody elephants doing inside your rifle?"
"Making trunk calls, sir?"

Fork and spoon
Description of the collar dot worn by infantrymen.

Fox-hole
Where vixens hang out. Also, trench deep enough for a soldier to stand and fire his rifle.

FBO
Full Battle Order. What a soldier has to bring along in case of war. Does not include Walkman.

GSO
General Staff Officer. Also, Girls Supply Officer at army parties.

Gabra
Panic or be confused.

Gabra king
A perpetual bundle of nerves.

Hammer
To pressure someone or make trouble for him.

Havoc
To create trouble. Describes those who have little regard for authority.

Helicopter

The Chinese-educated soldier. The story goes that a Chinese-educated recruit, when asked what school he came from, answered "Chinese helucated," which went down in the army annals as Chinese helicopter. Nowadays, extremely inarticulate soldiers are called Blue Thunder (named after the film and TV series about a super advanced US chopper).

Hew

(Hokkien) Interested. "No hew" is thus to disregard instructions or orders.

Horrigible

Describes person worse than horrible.

Idle

Lazy.

Idle king

Lazy slob.

Indian chief

Person appointed to head a section or platoon.

Iron picket

Angled length of metal used in field training to either build bashas or fences; usually heavily greased after use to prevent rusting.

Jerry can

So can I. Container for drinking water brought on field training.

Kang he kia

(Hokkien) Small fish; ikan bilis. Derogatory reference to a lance corporal's stripe.

Kiasu

(Hokkien) One who's scared of failing. Describes the breed which will not dare to do anything for fear of getting into trouble; or one who is overcautious.
Example: Kiasu soldiers wishing to pass their eye test usually memorise the entire eye chart the night before.

Khoon

(Hokkien) Sleep.

Khoon king

(Hokkien) Mr Dunlopillo.

Liam keng

(Hokkien) To recite prayers. Describes officers and NCOs who repeat and repeat instructions to their men. Describes officers and NCOs who repeat and repeat instructions to their men.

Liak bo kiu

(Hokkien) Catch no ball. Nothing has been understood at all. Usually whispered aloud at the end of long sonorous lectures.

Lobo

Acronym for lazy old bastard; the guy who is the odd one out and gets to miss training. Properly, LOB-left out of battle.

Lost

Blur or blank.

M&D

Malingering and default. Doctor's prescription that could make a soldier feigning sickness really ill.

Ngeow

(Hokkien) Cat. Used to describe superior who is unnecessarily tough or strict. Also applies to fusspots who demand their way.

On
To be alert and conscientious. Kiasu soldiers are usually on.

On charge
To be up for punishment.

On the ball
To be on; one who never misses a move.

On the wrong ball
To make right moves at the wrong time.

PGO
Police General Orders. Describes an officer who sticks to the books.

POP
Passing-out parade; where soldiers are expected to graduate, not faint.

PTI
Physical Training Instructor. The types who aim to make Rambos out of all recruits.

PT kit

Vest, shorts and canvas shoes-standard attire for physical training.

ROD

Run-out date. The date upon which NS men complete their army stint, a date they can recall more readily than their own birthdays.

ROD mood

Feeling of euphoria that overcomes most NS men when they feel freedom is close. Symptoms are a marked decrease in kiasu-ness. Some soldiers are possessed by the ROD mood from the day of their enlistment.

Regular

Smaller than large. Also, name for soldiers who make a career in the army.

Sabo

Short for sabotage. To make trouble for someone or to jeopardise his position.

Sabo king

Unfriendly term for the poor guy who inadvertently gets his mates into trouble.

Sampai tua

(Malay) Until old age. Describes a soldier with no future of advancement in the army.

Screw upside down

Painful. To be punished or reprimanded severely.

Selekeh

(Malay) Sloppy or untidy.

Seow eh

(Hokkien) Mad one. Term of endearment for buddy.

Si peh

(Hokkien) Literally, dead father; the ultimate. Used as prefix to place emphasis on description.
Example: Si peh ngeow.

Skive

To escape duty.

Sian

(Hokkien) Bored or lethargic. Popularly prefixed with si peh.

Siong

(Hokkien) Tough. Should also be prefixed with si peh.

Specky
Nickname for bespectacled soldier.

Stand-by-bed
Inspection of soldier's bed and personal belongings in the barracks.

Suka-suka
(Malay) As you wish. Describes couldn't-care-less attitude of some soldiers.

Switch on
To be on the ball.

Switch off
To not bother at all.

Take
Usually followed by a number. If a soldier is told to take seven, it means that he has to do seven duties.

Take cover
To hide.

Terok
(Malay) Tough; like siong.

Than chia

(Hokkien) Livelihood. Refers to regulars who depend on the army for a living.

Thia boh

(Hokkien) Hear nothing; as in liak bo kiu.

Tiok beh pio

(Hokkien) To strike lottery. Commonly used when one checks the guard duty list on the notice board and spots one's name.

Togok

(Malay) To guzzle. Used to describe drinking sessions.

Wake up your ideas

Scolding reserved for blur kings and idle kings.

What the fish

Euphemism for "What the f– ".

Wowo

Yeh-yeh, I love you more than I can say. Also, wash out. Descriptive word for when a soldier completely misses the target during shooting practices.

Wowo king

One who misses more times than anyone else.

Yaya

Nonchalant; also one who acts tough.
Example: "Who gave you permission to smoke? You don't simply yaya around here, understand?"

DON'T DRINK THAT WATER!!!
HAH! YOU'LL NEVER GET A DROP FROM MY JERRY CAN!

...NOT WHEN THERE'S PLENTY MORE BEHIND YOU!!!

Let's Get Physical

Rumour had it that they sent the overweight soldiers to Kilo Company. Those with hearing deficiencies ended up in Echo Company.

Needless to say, I purchased a pair of green leotards when I was told that I was to be posted to Foxtrot Company.

Whatever one's physical limitations, the SAF endeavours to build up your stamina, self-confidence and physique. If you're lucky, you end up with all three. Most lie in sick bay with sprained ankles and bruised egos.

For a great number of NS men, 5 BX sessions were tantamount to commando suicide missions. Yet, with fervent determination, these ambitious young men were soon able to execute star-jumps and touch toes without damaging the seams of their PT shorts.

But in the army, there are always new heights to conquer. A fact we discovered with much alarm.

Just when we had learned to live with 5 BX, they brought on running sessions. I think we did not protest hard enough when told to wear uniforms and those calamitous boots instead of shorts and Nike sneakers.

We did the obligatory warm-up exercises with mournful spirits, convinced we would spend the rest of our lives in wheelchairs.

I made a last desperate attempt to make my fears known to the relevant authorities.

"Cannot lah, really cannot!" I screeched. The young officer showed no compassion.

It was no use. Remembering that in one episode of *Teenage Mutant Ninja Turtles* on TV, my heroes pulled through a punishing experience by ceaselessly repeating "mind over matter" in their heads, I applied the same strategy.

For a while it worked. I could feel the wind fuel my enthusiasm as I rushed headward into the fore muttering, "Mind over matter, mind over matter … "

I was still muttering those cryptic words when the medics picked me up in a stretcher 10 minutes later.

"Stamina lah, Joe," lectured the PTI. "You got no stamina!" He prescribed a series of stamina building exercises for me.

This was it. I could just see myself secretly training while everyone else was asleep, practising my body-building manoeuvres in the dead of night. This 40-kilo weakling would turn into a hunk of ruthless muscle by the time the running test came.

I'd seen it done before. Jackie Chan, Sylvester Stallone, Jean-Claude Van Damme – they all did it the same way. My cup ranneth over with gloat.

Night after night, waiting till the platoon was soundly snoring, I crept out into the dewy training field and went through my routine.

I ran on the spot. I did push-ups. I skipped.

I stretched. I inhaled deeply. I caught pneumonia.

On the day of the test, I watched the runners from my wheelchair.

After my recovery, I joined the platoon in yet another dastardly piece of physical training – the obstacle course.

The first thing they make you do here is climb a seven-foot wall. I offered to do 20 pushups in exchange for a ladder, but the corporals would not budge.

Neither would the wall. I clawed, crept and cursed, but nothing happened. In a final act of desperation, I scaled it. That the PTI boosted me from behind is not really relevant to this story. What matters is I found out what lay behind the wall. Ten more bloody obstacles.

Alaska may have its petrified forests, but Singapore will forever have its petrified recruits. Fear not only gnawed at my vitals, it chewed heartily at my every limb.

"Mind over matter?" I squeaked to myself.

I was a figure of perfect inelegance as I sought to

cross the Parallel Bars and swing over the Window. A gangly bundle of terror as I shimmied my way up the Rope and tiptoed over Jacob's Ladder, I was finding within me hitherto unknown reservoirs of pain and panic.

Those were the days.

PTIs, being men of initiative, also took time to explore areas of activity that lay beyond the borders of standard exercises and good taste.

One of these fringe events encompassed different styles of walking. Initially, there was much excitement as we welcomed the prospect of having 2.5-km runs replaced by afternoon walks and morning strolls. Alas alack, this was not to be.

The walks the instructors had in mind were something else altogether. They wanted us to duck walk, monkey run, leopard crawl and perform other forms of exotic movement.

These exercises were usually conducted early in the morning, after breakfast and area cleaning, and before the day's training started.

Clearly etched into my memory is that fateful morning when I pocketed a hard-boiled egg from breakfast and hurried along happily for the PT lesson.

As luck would have it, we started out with the duck walk down the slope. Barely four waddles later, the egg nipped out of my back pocket.

RECRUIT! WHERE IS YOUR LOG?!
RIGHT HERE, SIR! DECEMBER 13...

Everyone stopped dead in his tracks. No one said a word as they watched that solitary egg roll around uncertainly before accelerating its way downhill.

When the egg finally completed its breathtaking performance, the whole platoon turned slowly to face me. The amazement had not left their faces. I, too, was dumbfounded.

Someone rang for the medical officer. To this day, I never found out if he had sent over the proctologist as a joke.

But I soon put the incident behind me. I had to. What loomed ahead in my never-ending test of physical endurance was impossible to ignore – a massive tree-trunk tossed around in the name of fitness and fun.

Welcome to log PT! What one smart aleck called the nymphomaniac's supreme fantasy. In log PT, a small group of soldiers perform exercises with a log that's 5 metres long, 30 centimetres wide and weighs a kiloton.

Merely lifting it brought you one step closer to hernia. You can imagine how enthused we were about running around the field with it, swinging it and tossing it in the air. This was lethal business. One false move and your head might be permanently displaced.

The log PT lesson climaxed with the soldiers holding the instrument of torture erect while one of us climbed to the top. Thrill of the day.

I have since spent many sleepless nights wondering about men who labour long hours devising ways through which soldiers might suffer at PT lessons. Do these men breathe the same air we do? What in heaven's name could induce human minds to formulate such dark deeds?

I have no answers. Only a sincere wish that these men be soundly tapped on the head by 10 PT logs before they come up with more ideas.

Please Don't Rain On My Parade

At first I couldn't figure out what was missing. There I was, standing at attention with the rest of the recruits for our very first muster parade, when my instincts told me in no uncertain terms that something was awfully wrong.

I looked left, right, front, up and down. My nervous platoon mates thought a command had been given for our 5 BX neck exercises, and quickly decided to follow suit.

So while the flag was slowly being raised, the entire body of men in Platoon 4, Foxtrot Company were earnestly rotating their heads in silent, clockwise motion.

I believe all our heads would have rolled if the RSM had spotted us. But as luck would have it, we were positioned at the rear of the parade and only served to confuse Platoons 3 and 5.

Anyway, it was while this rotary routine was in progress that I figured out what was missing-rousing band music.

It was so obvious. National Day parades in school,

on the Padang, on TV, all had this gungho ensemble of bandsmen providing ambience. A parade had to have music. Remember Chingay?

This revelation upset me so much that my entire body system refused to obey all subsequent drill commands for the next three days.

So it was that at drill practice, while the rest of the men snapped to attention, I was still standing at ease, with my feet exactly thirty-seven-and-a-half centimetres apart.

Now if my body kept still while the platoon marched, we may have averted disaster. Instead, the NCOs were confronted with this weak-kneed recruit marching down the parade square like a crude caricature of a cheap slut, with hands neatly positioned behind him. Until then, the only person the corporals had seen walking that way was Kevin Costner – and only after he'd dismounted a fat horse.

Meanwhile, my rebellious lower limbs clomped relentlessly forward. Then backward. Have you ever attempted a *ke-belakang pusing* (about-turn) on the move with your feet apart? That day, my knee caps stabbed two soldiers in their kidneys.

By this time, my drill instructor had broken down completely. I fully sympathised. I was forcibly dragged off the parade square, my legs still swinging to a beat of their own.

Specialists later diagnosed that I was suffering from an uncommon case of acute rhythmic deficiency. They put me in a padded room where they continuously piped in all three volumes of *The Complete Marches of Sousa*.

It cured my problem but left me with recurring nightmares where I was pursued by cellists from the Boston Symphony Orchestra conducted by a famous fashion designer. I am sure there was some profound message somewhere in there, but at that time, it was just bizarre. Not to mention tiring.

It was in this untoward manner that I was initiated into the finer points of army parades. Muster parades, staff parades, passing-out parades, National Day parades, SAF Day parades, and change parades.

Change parades are a totally different kettle of fish. Here, the soldier is subjected to great psychological pressure to test his reflexes and responses.

The idea is to have the soldier change from one uniform into another in the shortest space of time. For example, you start out with drill uniform, move to PT kit, then progress to Full Battle Order.

It sounded like fun. But this sentiment was very rapidly erased from our minds when we found out that the change parades took place on the parade square, while our uniforms were back in our barracks.

The first stage is straightforward enough. You were

ordered to fall in in parade dress. It is only when you are told "Change to PT kit!" that the frenzied chaos begins.

You dash upstairs to your barracks, start undoing those mile-long bootlaces, tear the boots off, then the socks, undo the belt, unbutton the fly, take off the pants, unbutton the shirt, take off the shirt, slip into PT shorts, throw on a vest, put on the socks again and jump into canvas shoes.

Downstairs, they are already falling into position. By the time you hurtle down the four flights of stairs, the others are already running back to the barracks for the next change.

In my family, I have always been the slowest. The whole gang would be finishing their breakfast and I would still be trying to raise myself from a supine position. Going out for dinner, I would be the one still fumbling with mismatched buttons while everyone was reading the menu.

I am the sort that takes a meticulously ordered and leisurely approach to life. Into this scheme of things, I could not fit a military practice calculated to stimulate the individual's reflexive prowess.

In other words, I did not excel in change parades.

The average change parade time was documented at two minutes. I took 15 – and forgot to put on my glasses. In the process, I ended up following Bravo Company for a blood donation.

Half a pint later, I realised my mistake and staggered back to my own company line.

For the safety of those in my proximity, change parades were subsequently abolished.

Welcome to the Pressure Dome

I once had a goldfish named Sushi. She swam merrily around in her goldfish bowl for a full week before she leapt out and died on my parquet floor.

At that point in time – I was 14 – I could not comprehend what drove poor Sushi to that dramatic conclusion. It was the first week in NS that I understood. I realised what had caused Sushi all that pain.

Not until you are thrown into a tiny room chockful of soldier boys can you fully understand the impact of living in a goldfish bowl.

Your every move is monitored by umpteen pairs of *kay poh* eyes. Your nervous fidget raises an eyebrow somewhere across the room. You cough and four people look up in disgust. Under such conditions, flatulence becomes a real liability.

The first night in my new quarters, I caused much consternation among the more conservative members with my flannel pyjamas. It had not crossed my mind that Mickey Mouse prints were not the norm in most

Singaporean homes. I cursed my brother – who bought me the pyjamas – in Japanese and quickly hid the matching bedroom slippers.

It was a tough experience, the first night in the barracks. No one tucked me in, no one offered to make me a cup of Ovaltine.

I began to worry.

Would I sleep with my mouth open? Would I make lewd suggestive noises in my sleep? Would my clothes fall into salacious disarray in the middle of the night?

The uneasy questions tumbled on and on in my head. Oh, to be remembered as The Recruit Who Snored in B Flat Minor. My piano teacher would have the fits.

The ceiling fan wound around weakly in a tizzy of sympathetic confusion. I must have looked as sorry as the soiled socks and the flaccid underwear draped over the bedrails.

Would any of these strange room-mates sleep-walk and – God forbid – trip and fall into my bed? My panic accelerated as the minutes ticked loudly away. The made-in-China alarm clock had a strong sense of presence.

Somewhere in the night, a toilet flushed.

I peered to the right of me. The Indian boy with the rash scratched his unmentionables. I peered to the left of me. The fat Eurasian boy with the lisp was still trying to count himself to sleep.

"One thouthandth and thix, one thouthandth and theven … "

I thimply thouldn't thleep.

Barrack life affords no one privacy. By the end of the second week, everyone in the room knew which direction I brushed my teeth, the size of my briefs, the amount in my POSB account, and the exact location of my birthmark.

But barracks have also generated some lighter moments. Now and then, a nerd would try to rally some camaraderie by initiating a sing-along session. At which point someone would whip out a guitar (MINDEF makes sure the guitar players are evenly distributed) and a pirated song book.

Now the guitar players. Most only know tunes by the Bee Gees and John Denver. And everyone in the barrack room will try to sound like the Bee Gees and John Denver, whining through their noses until someone stops breathing altogether.

If the next generation of Singaporeans is born with sinus defects, they have these sing-song sessions to blame.

The corporals usually make their protocol rounds on such occasions. They come around and nod their heads slowly like head doctors visiting patients; tease the fat guy with the flat feet ("So, cannot dance like Michael Jackson, ah?"); tell stories about how much

BED-
TIME
STORIES

tougher their training was ("During my time … "); and tap the weaklings on the head. (It cleared my dandruff within three weeks.)

There was much to do in the barracks in between the singing and the diplomatic visits. A little notice board kept each one's cleaning duties rostered. A calendar-usually scenic shots of Japan or Switzerland in winter-kept tabs on our progress through army life.

In a fit of joy, some officers would announce a Cleanest Barrack Line Competition and send our lives into great turmoil.

Posters of Hongkong movie starlets wearing small towels would miraculously appear on the notice board. The less time we had to clean up the barracks, the smaller the towels. You see, we believed in the power of distraction.

At the appointed time of the inspection, the officers would troop in, cast a civil eye over the room, start to make notes about dust on the window sill when, suddenly, the Amy Yip poster would be noticed.

End of inspection.

For demonstrating a sense of aestheticism we won.

Later, the swimsuit poster was graciously accepted by the Officers' Mess. They declined my offer of the bedroom slippers.

Everything But the Girls

Save for middle-aged spinsters who operate the canteen, women are not commonly encountered on army premises during basic military training. Which explains why girlfriends are really appreciated on weekends. Such are the laws of deprivation.

Without even making an actual appearance, girlfriends can make their presence felt in camp.

Recruits with girlfriends are a culture unto themselves. They talk different, walk different and behave strange.

Like crusaders in search of the Holy Grail, these recruits will journey tirelessly across the army compound and canteen in hope of locating a working public phone.

Once found, the joyous news is beamed to others in the flock. Devotees of every colour and creed then come forth, willingly divesting themselves of their hard-earned 10-cent coins in a moving display of faith.

This ritual is traditionally performed in its entirety

in the evenings, though it can occasionally be carried out during lunch- or tea-breaks.

Avoid interrupting the devotee during this time. The emotional intensity with which a lovesick recruit conducts this communication exercise with the outside world is no trifling matter.

Attempts to disconnect the harmonious union of caller and callee have been known to result in violence.

Burnt weekends and Valentine's Day duty can also drive romancing recruits insane. The prospect of not being able to spend a meaningful evening with the love of one's life can be shattering to a hormonally active 18-year-old.

As for me, I never attached that much significance to the telephone. Not after my mother hung up on me when I called her one night asking if we could all emigrate to Australia before my obstacle test.

It was then that I suspected I was an adopted child.

Platoon functions are another thing in which girlfriends figure strongly. Many of us were convinced that these get-togethers were organised with the sole purpose of allowing socially-inept corporals and sergeants a chance to scrutinise women at close proximity without getting arrested. To those of us without steady girlfriends, these social events were a nightmare.

To avoid having further aspersions cast upon our already doubtful manhoods, we set out to secure dates.

Sisters, female cousins and ex-classmates suddenly assumed a new relevance in our lives.

Some of us went through class photos in school annuals in search of possible prey. Others began paying friendly visits to long-lost aunts and uncles in hope of stumbling upon hitherto unnoticed young women in the household.

My best friend tried persuading his pen-pal from Kuala Lumpur to catch a bus down for the occasion, promising a romantic dinner on the sandy shores of our tropical island, where she would be courted by some of the most dashing young hunks in the region. She wrote back and told him where he could shove his writing instrument.

We scoured the country for compassionate women. The more sympathetic the women, the higher their demands. They were especially expensive in the Orchard vicinity.

Fellow recruits with eligible sisters became instant hits. Everybody wanted to be their best friends. We polished their boots, cleaned their rifles, made their beds and washed their underwear in a move to win their trust and their sisters.

But there were just too many contenders. A total of 26 luckless souls angling for eight sisters. We did our best to plead our individual plights, but it proved a difficult dilemma to resolve. In the end, we all gathered at the canteen and conducted a lucky draw. My best friend won a date with Kelvin's anorexic sister. I won a disposable Gillette razor with twin blades.

The platoon function itself proved an anticlimax after the gruelling manoeuvres we had put ourselves through. We ate burnt sausages and chicken wings in Pasir Ris, mingled self-consciously, and took turns singing *Unchained Melody* on the Pioneer karaoke set.

The women gave patronising smiles, declined our beer; nibbled on potato chips, slapped a few mosquitoes, and made silent vows never to come near army boys again.

Three of the eight sisters wanted to go home. The rest joined the party in the next chalet. And the two social escorts insisted on having XO.

I was fortunate. The middle-aged canteen operator brought her own drinks.

Enemy in Front, Charge!

If the weatherman forecasts thundery showers in scattered parts of the island, you can be sure that the army will conduct training there. It never fails.

Anyhow, field training is one of the most exciting things about NS, no matter what the weatherman says.

It is here that one puts to practice all the wisdom and knowledge accumulated from lessons in basic soldiering. One learns to apply the golden rules of behaviour in the field: no littering, no spitting, no chewing gum, no dialects, and always queue. And where possible, find true love, get married, and have at least three children.

Then there's camouflage. How to make yourself blend in with the natural surroundings and avoid detection by unfriendly forces. The trick is to disguise oneself with grass, leaves and small potted plants. Cactus is inadvisable.

Some soldiers have an inborn flair for camouflage. With a few deftly applied sprigs they recede into oblivion.

I do not have this facility. I tend to radiate when placed beside lallang. I tried my best at camouflage, but always ended up looking more like a fruit stall than an infantryman. This was caused by my habit of gravitating towards the use of banana leaves and fresh papaya.

I also found that corporals seldom appreciate orchids on a soldier's helmet, however skilfully arranged.

Anyhow, once suitably disguised as plants, we would march in formation as we trekked cautiously across a terrain splotched with pig and vegetable farms.

The enemy came in many forms. One which always caught us unawares was the soft-drinks seller. These hawkers were the downfall of many an NS man. Hard-earned pay dwindled at the sight of these tempters.

"Coca-Cola, Seven-up, Sarsi, Orleng! Lai ah, lai ah!" cried those guileless voices. They always knew where to find us. One suspects they are on MINDEF' s mailing list.

Attacks and ambushes were what livened up the dreary routines of many raw soldiers. However much we detested strenuous exercises, there was something perversely enjoyable about charging up hills and screaming "bang-bang-bang!"

True, we had blank rounds to fire on many occasions, but nothing quite replaced the energetic yells of lusty 18-year-olds.

The fun stopped when it came to carrying casualties. Here, soldiers have to carry to safety their mates "wounded" in the encounter with the enemy. "Casualties" were nominated by the NCOs, who never failed to pick soldiers that looked like aspiring sumo wrestlers.

Bearing the weight of these humongous members of our race upon our scrawny frames, we tried to move in the desired direction.

"Come on, run! Don't walk, run!" hollered the NCOs.

They should have been satisfied that we even managed to stand up. Nonetheless, we plodded on, making mental notes to ourselves to raise fat children. Let not our sons suffer the humiliation of their hunchbacked fathers.

By the end of the exercises, many of us developed backaches, cramps, rash and dehydration. Some went into fits of manic depression at the sight of obese uniformed personnel.

Understandably, this had a demoralising effect on a few of the chubbier soldiers. Upon completion of NS, they retreated to obscure parts of the island where they and their families are rumoured to be selling soft drinks.

They bear no ill will towards MINDEF. As long as they remain on the mailing list.

A-Camping We Will Go

The excitement of overnight camping peaks during one's school days. Once your student days are over, the prospect of spending a few nights under the stars quickly loses its appeal.

This phenomenon might be traced to NS.

Unlike schoolboy camps at Changi, Pasir Ris or East Coast Park, where frolicsome activities are encouraged, field camps in the army are serious events conducted to test the individual's survival instincts.

It is during the three-month Basic Military Training course that an NS man learns about the vital differences between the two types of camping. Unfortunately, I had no prior knowledge of this important piece of information. When told that we would be embarking on a field camp the following week, I was elated and worked myself up to a feverish pitch of excitement that weekend.

My father bought me a Pictionary set. I borrowed my brother's ukulele and *Hawaiian Hits* songbook. As a fail-safe, I brought along the portable cassette-player and my entire collection of Madonna tapes.

I packed my bicycle shorts, Esprit T-shirts, sunglasses and suntan lotion. As it couldn't fit, I was forced to leave my deck chair behind. I returned to the barrack line that night in a state of euphoria. This was the life!

We left for the campsite the next day at 7 a.m. When I observed that the three-tonners weren't heading in the general direction of the East Coast Lagoon, I had a nagging suspicion that something was not quite right.

We arrived in the middle of the Mandai Forest Reserve at 8:30 a.m. I managed to suppress a strong urge to sob.

We were ordered to start building our bashas. Me and my basha-mate did a lightning survey of the area to see which spot we might want to rest our vulnerable-bodies that night.

The ground conditions didn't meet our exacting requirements. We wanted some place dry, uniformly even, not too hard to sleep on, and with a pleasing view of the reservoir at sunset.

The officers had other ideas. The site they allocated for our basha was muddy, uneven, and faced the toilet.

We were most reasonable soldiers. We did as we were told. It was a better alternative to doing guard duty over Chinese New Year.

Having pitched our tent, we tried to make the abode cosy. Unfortunately, there was no convenient outlet to plug in the bedside lamp. Still, we both agreed the scatter cushions added a nice touch.

We dug a little trough around the basha. This would serve as a drain for rain water in case of thundery showers. This trench would deftly divert the rushing rivulets of rain, when it came, into the neighbouring bashas.

Diabolical.

On the perimeter of our tent, we sprinkled sulphur. The yellow powder keeps away snakes, frogs, scorpions and other creepy crawlies that could nibble one's ear at night.

At last, our pitiful tent was ready for habitation. Up until this point, it had not really occurred to me that I was actually going to sleep in it. But, when night fell, my destiny became inescapable.

My basha-mate was not someone to whom you could apply the term "svelte" by any stretch of the imagination. He's the sort that could effectively cause an eclipse of the sun if he went parachuting.

Meanwhile, he was trying to crawl into the basha without demolishing it. After what seemed like an eternity, he succeeded in getting himself inside. At which point the basha looked like an inflated circus tent.

From a distance, one could be forgiven for thinking that a whale had been forcibly pinned to the floor with a ground sheet, so sharply did the waterproof material adhere to the contours of his body.

There was no way anything could have squeezed inside with him. I sprinkled sulphur over myself and laid down to rest beside the snoring blimp.

Thankfully it didn't rain all through the field camp. I once had a friend who was washed into the reservoir during an evening drizzle. His empty water bottle kept him afloat until help arrived.

I never got to sing my Hawaiian songs. And it took me four days to convince the doctor that my strange pallor was due to sulphur and not jaundice.

My entire perspective on camping changed with that experience. To this day I would rather spend a weekend in a cardboard box than brave the elements of nature from within the confines of a tent.

Nothing could be more awful than having to sleep in a flimsy ground-sheet tent. Or so I thought. I had yet to be introduced to defence camps.

Defence camps do not take place in Mandai Forest Reserve or East Coast Lagoon. They are carried out on hilly terrain. Soldiers do not build bashas and sleep on the ground. They dig trenches and sleep in the ground.

My only previous experience with digging was weeding flower beds in primary school during

compulsory gardening periods. And now they expected me to dig a trench big enough to accommodate two full-grown men? The mind boggled.

I made generous monetary offers to the muscle-bound members of our platoon in the hope that they would demonstrate some of their skills in advanced gardening. They merely kicked sand in my face.

I was left with no choice. I put on my gloves, clenched the changkul and dug. The Angel of Exhaustion watched over me as I toiled.

I figured that if O Lan could do it in *The Good Earth,* surely a strapping young soldier like me could not fail. But O Lan probably had bigger biceps. I crumbled in a sorry heap by midday.

The army was determined that I carry on. The corporals splashed cold water on me, rubbed Tiger Balm on my pulse points, and also threatened to neuter me if I didn't regain consciousness.

As I had no great desire to sing in the Vienna Boys' Choir, I decided to give the trench another shot.

Relentlessly I flailed at the unyielding earth. Flail, flail, flail. How I finally completed that trench remains a complete mystery to me to this day.

Some say the subconscious mind has a hidden power, a strength to overcome what is seen to be an impossibility. I say threats of violent bodily harm motivate men just as effectively.

So we dug our trenches, toppled into them and passed out. By day our bodies went through the motions of basic soldiering as we set out on recce missions, patrols, ambushes, and the inevitable attacks.

By night our bodies surrendered to the forces of gravity and turned into tired lumps that clung tenaciously to the earth from which we came.

Eminent psychologists have likened the whole experience to the embryonic state – the idea of returning to the womb. It probably explains why I was overcome by a craving for pickled cucumber and experienced morning sickness for the next two weeks.

Halt! Who Goes There?

So what is it about guard duty that strikes terror into the hearts of all NS men?

As a novice soldier, I couldn't fathom the hue and cry that accompanied the mere mention of the phrase "do guard."

The instructions that I was given on my first guard assignment seemed harmless enough: patrol the perimeter fence for two hours. If you spot some one suspicious, shout "Halt! Who goes there?" Having established that it's no one of significance, proceed with the patrolling until the next detail relieves you. I'd seen it done in war movies and on TV. I was itching to play real-life hero.

I set out on my first shift that night with gusto. I tiptoed along the fence to see if I might flush out secret agents from their hide-out in the shadows.

I had visions of myself capturing a three-man Communist mission attempting to sabotage our drinking water with Harpic. My folks would be so pleased. A medal to display on the TV cabinet.

I was nursing such heroic ambitions when I fell into the monsoon drain. After checking to see that no major parts of my anatomy had been inconvenienced, I climbed out. My folks would have to be content with a desk calendar.

By the end of my first hour on duty, I was enlightened. I knew what it was about guard duty that was so intolerable.

Boredom.

Guard duty was just so unbelievably boring. The seconds didn't go tick-tick-tick. They went tick. Pause. Tick. Pause. Tick.

One could develop wrinkles waiting for the minutes to pass. Guards on patrol look at their watches every 30 seconds, convinced the minute hand is moving backwards.

For those on sentry duty, things are no better. The sentry guard's task is to stand motionless in his sentry box. Period. He just stands there, guarding. If he's lucky, an officer passes by and he gets a chance to salute. Otherwise he just spends two hours staring into space and periodically shifting his weight from one leg to the other. He, too, steals a disbelieving glance at his watch regularly.

In between shifts, the guards return to the guard room. These supposed rest areas are about as jolly as a morgue. Bleary-eyed soldiers either sit glumly at the table and watch their fingernails grow or try to sleep on creaky beds while keeping their boots off the tacky sheets.

I discovered abject boredom to be almost tangible. No wonder weekend duty is feared like the plague. A 12-hour duty is already interminable.

There is basic guard duty. And there is advanced guard duty. The latter is available at SAFTI, the army's training institute located at an end of the world called Pasir Laba.

At SAFTI, guard duty becomes a veritable challenge. Especially when you are sent to guard the Magazine.

My naturally active and imaginative mind construed this to be a large important library stocked with military periodicals like *Pioneer*, *Soldier's Digest* and *Grenades Illustrated.*

Ha-ha. It turned out to be an ammunition dump. Dark and creepy. But the worst was yet to come.

I was assigned to stand guard at one of the watchtowers. In the movies, isn't it always the watchtower guard who gets knocked off first? Armed with this cheering nugget of information, I made my way up the narrow overgrown path to my assigned tower.

The wind made sinister swishy sounds in the trees. I swallowed loudly, clutched the phosphorescent crucifix to my chest, and bravely continued my journey.

WHEN I SAID 'SPRAY THEM', I MEANT WITH THIS!

I lied. It wasn't the prospect of getting picked off by an enemy sniper that chilled my bones. It was that notorious story about the ghost that stalked one of the towers. The trouble was, I couldn't remember which tower. All I knew was that this unseen entity sometimes sought to amuse itself by noisily climbing the metal rungs of the ladder that led up to the 10-metre tower. It usually paid scant attention to the startled guard's frantic cries of "Who goes there?"

On some occasions, this night visitor took to scratching the underside of the tower box in long, deliberate strokes. By this time, most guards had passed out cold.

My impressionable young mind bursting with these horror stories, I climbed up the ladder. I couldn't remember any appropriate prayers to recite, so made do with Christmas carols.

I got to the top of the ladder by the time I had finished *Silent Night, Holy Night.* I stepped into the tower box and looked around me. I was surrounded by a shadowy mass of tree tops. Black and suggestive. I decided to continue singing for a while longer.

There was a slight problem. The only other carol I knew by heart was *Jingle Bells.* It struck me as rather unsuitable for my purpose, but in desperation I sang it anyway.

For the next two hours, I broke into song every time I heard a twig break, an insect call, a branch move. At the slightest provocation, I sang *Jingle Bells.* Every now and then I threw in a few hallelujahs for good measure.

Nothing happened to me that night. I passed an uneventful evening and lived to tell of my experiences at the watchtower.

I frequently look back on that night and see the event as a ritual wherein my manhood and courage were put to the test. I failed both.

Should I Sign On?

One burning question that seldom appears in the consciousness of the average NS man is whether to sign on as a regular.

But there have occurred from time to time isolated cases of NS men who, in the course of their compulsory service, make the decision to stay on as career soldiers.

The SAF regulars have distinct advantages over the irregulars in terms of pay, privileges and prospects.

But how do you know if you're what the army needs? Are you truly suitable for a career in soldiering? Might not your strong affinity for the army be influenced by a leaning towards bondage and discipline?

Make doubly sure that green is your scene before you sign on that dotted line. Take the simple "Does the Army Want A Man Like Me?" quiz.

The "Does the Army Want a Man Like Me?" Quiz

1. As a child, I enjoyed playing with:
   a) plastic toy soldiers and tanks
   b) the baby-sitter
   c) electricity

2. I believe that the only way to run a large organisation efficiently is through:
   a) rigidly enforced discipline
   b) luck
   c) hoola-hoops

3. I feel that a sound mind is the product of:
   a) well-balanced physical training
   b) well-balanced hi-fi speakers
   c) well-balanced athletic supporters

4. I only watch TV if:
   a) it's a documentary on The Gulf War or World War II
   b) Diana Koh wears Gianni Versace
   c) it's a Sony

5. When watching the National Day Parade on TV, I feel:
    a) left out
    b) like experimenting with make-up
    c) like abstaining from red meat on public holidays

6. I spend most weekends:
    a) taking refresher courses at the Outward Bound School
    b) abusing durian sellers
    c) unconscious

7. In a group, I am usually the most:
    a) vocal
    b) under-nourished
    c) voluptuous

8. Most of my close friends are:
    a) uniformed personnel
    b) graduate women
    c) registered with the Middle Road Clinic

9. When meeting strangers, I usually:
    a) hold my stomach in and my chest out
    b) take their temperatures
    c) remark how closely they resemble various vegetables

10. When relaxing, I enjoy listening to:
    a) SAF Day speeches
    b) Julio Iglesias' Greatest Hits Volume II
    c) the air-conditioner

11. The word "pip" brings to my mind:
    a) an SAF second lieutenant
    b) English literature for A-levels
    c) a small delicate operation normally performed on male cats

12. When I see a VIP state car drive past, my first reaction is to:
    a) salute
    b) argue with the bus driver
    c) take down the car number and buy 4-D

13. If I have a son, I would want him to:
    a) join the Air Force
    b) mud-wrestle with female midgets
    c) do his own laundry on weekends

14. The best thing about NS:
    a) is the food
    b) is one's ROD
    c) has yet to make itself known to me

15. The worst thing about NS:
    a) is wimpy soldiers
    b) is the food
    c) having to actually do it

How you scored

If more than half your choices were (a), you were not only born to be a soldier, you were probably a famous dictator in your previous life.

If more than half of your choices were (b), you have little attraction to the army. You should try and concentrate on improving your living room furniture.

If more than half of your choices were (c), you should be locked up before you become a security risk.

Relax, Don't Do It

NS is not all work and no play. In between the arduous hours on the field and the wearisome guard duties, NS men have been known to take breathers. They have even been seen relaxing.

Those with a preference for cerebral stimulation try to engage in informal discussions on genetic theories and nuclear disarmament. However, such sessions seldom go very far as the total combined IQ of the participants often does not exceed two digits.

I relaxed occasionally during my NS. I spent time playing Game Boy. Gave lessons. My platoon sergeant conducted microwave cooking classes. Members of our platoon who were less nimble with their hands took up target spitting. This class was conducted by a former bus driver who could hit moving targets from up to five metres. He represented his depot in the 1985 Target Spitting Championships and won.

On its part, the SAF also encouraged seasonal bouts of relaxation. Soldiers in some camps were fortunate enough to have swimming sessions included in their timetables. The army not only supplied standard black cotton trunks but also paid the admission charges and promised to cover funeral expenses in case of drowning.

But the most publicised form of relaxation in the army is the Road Show. Before its proper inception, these shows comprised small-scale exhibitions of tracks made by different armoured vehicles. They were not a resounding success and were later replaced by the variety programme.

Today, SAF Road Shows are synonymous with lively entertainment. In addition to the songs, dances and skits put up by the Music and Drama Company, the Road Show always features items by members of the host camp.

When the SAF Road Show came to our camp, an audition was held in our Company. We were strongly encouraged to volunteer. Those who did not would be sent to Marsiling on a TOPO march ... without maps. We fought tooth and nail to get into the audition.

Section 1 attempted a delightful little vignette based on one of Salman Rushdie' s more obscure works. It was deemed unsuitable as it made unsavoury references to the eating habits of diabetic lance corporals.

Section 2 went for mass appeal and did a rendition of the "Colonel Bogey March" from *Bridge Over the*

River Kwai in four-part harmony. They were selected but had to withdraw on the actual night when two of the soldiers developed mouth ulcers and couldn't whistle.

Section 3 contributed a folk dance. It was a simple, peasant routine with clumsy formations but pleasing to the unschooled eye. However, it was banned on the actual night when a vindictive member of Section 1 revealed that it was a fertility dance with sensitive political overtones.

I tried to convince my own section to do a rap version of *Dream of the Red Chamber,* but was overruled in favour of a fire-walking display. I had no violent objections until I learnt I had to lead the procession. Thankfully, the item never went on. We all had cold feet.

So we watched in semi envy as the other platoons charmed the audience with harmonica recitals, aerobics routines and two versions of *Count On Me, Singapore.*

The Music and Dance Company show was, as always, a treat. They sang songs that weren't restricted to only one octave and poured on the seductive tease in the dance numbers. Even the girls were good.

We put up stoically with the unavoidable sing-alongs, holding up cyclostyled song sheets to extol the virtues of Tanjong Katong yet another time.

Yes, soldiers do find time to relax somewhere along the way under any set of conditions. However rough, however tough.

So long as they don't have to sing *Chan Mali Chan*.

And So It Came to Pass

Legend has it that the first batch of NS recruits to complete their basic military training were so exhausted by the course that when they arrived for their graduation ceremony, they all promptly fainted on the parade square.

Hence the passing out parade.

Recruits look forward to the passing-out parade (or POP) because it gives them the feeling that their horrendous initiation into the military is over. It is that one day when they can stand tall, with stomachs in and chests out, and be amazed that they have not been hospitalised yet.

The parade heralded a new era. From bumbling greenhorn recruits, we had matured into bumbling greenhorn privates.

It was after this that the posting orders would arrive, and the new privates would all be assembled to find out where they would be sent to next.

While we all spoke in gruff voices about wanting to be tough-talking corporals and officers, secretly we longed to become clerks. The idea of sitting behind a desk with one's own telephone sent delicious tremors down our wobbly spines. Such was the power of the clerical persuasion.

We all felt we had charged up enough hills, marched enough routes, cleared enough obstacles and shot enough enemy soldiers to warrant a rest.

Surely the world at large could finally distinguish us men from the boys?

I guess not.

Looking around at our fellow soldiers at the parade, it wasn't hard to tell that many of us soft-bellied weaklings had only managed to become hard-bellied weaklings. You could tell the beef from the mincemeat. The real soldier stood out.

You know the type. Every graduating platoon has one hero. Ours was an all-tanned, all-correct, all-purpose soldier who lived and breathed the SAF code of honour. The one who excelled in the very things that the rest of us got suicidal over.

He was the model soldier. The kind who would probably play the lead in an SBC serial about a young man who sacrifices the woman he loves to pursue his uniformed vocation and ends up saving a fictitious ASEAN island from a coup d'etat.

He was the one who would queue piously at the bus stop on weekends while the rest of us rushed forward and trampled senior citizens with our combat boots. He gave blood with stoic dignity while the rest of us quivered, quaked and made obscene noises before passing out cold.

While the majority of us pimply 18-year-olds shuffled around cautiously on weak knees, he walked with confidence. He stood erect, and moved with pronounced, purposeful strides. This, however, could be attributed to tight underwear.

So it came as no surprise that he was the star of our platoon. After all, he shone in the marksmanship test, the obstacle test, the fieldcraft test, the running test, and still had time to wash his own socks and memorise the lyrics to 20 Sing Singapore songs in the four official languages.

He won Best Recruit, Best Runner, Best Marksman. I didn't even win Best Dressed. He took home the challenge shield and a cash prize.

I brought home a medium-sized hernia.

I'm Recalling You-oo-oo-oo!

What often terrifies women is picking up the phone in the middle of the night and hearing heavy breathing or a strange voice intimating lewd scenarios.

What terrifies army men is hearing a cold voice whisper "recall."

This phobia is most prevalent on Saturday nights. Out on the town, the soldier begins by showing sudden signs of despair if he catches sight of a public phone.

This phone fixation continues when he returns home, where he interrogates his mother about in-coming calls. By midnight, he calms down and tries to go to sleep. He puts on his Lionel Richie tape. Unfortunately, it plays *Hello.* He grows hysterical.

At 1:20 a.m., the phone rings. He leaps two feet off the mattress, hits the air-conditioner and accidentally depresses the high velocity button. His hair in instant disarray, he whisks out to answer the phone.

"Hello?" he asks, barely breathing. It is a wrong number. He responds in Hokkien with a graphic comment about the caller's mother.

Finally at 2 a.m., he gets his obscene phone call from camp.

"Recall, recall," he groans weakly to the sleeping household.

This is not a tale conjured up to alarm families who have members in the army. Rather it is a call for understanding towards individuals exhibiting symptoms of *recallis interruptus.*

In a recall, all members of a particular army camp are required to report back to base within a specified number of hours. Key personnel are given a shorter deadline, while ordinary soldiers usually have a longer time to make the trip back.

As not all soldiers have phones, the army also depends on other soldiers to physically pass on the message. The recall duty person thus finds himself trekking into outlying parts of the island looking for people.

And so I once found myself trekking to Punggol to inform three soldiers about a recall. The fact that I didn't drive was already a point in my disfavour. As my father flatly refused to drive me to some alien territory in the middle of the night, I was forced to use my brother's bike.

By the time I had pedalled my way from Bukit Timah to Punggol, I had barely time left on my deadline.

The roosters were beginning to crow as I negotiated my two-wheeler down the pitch dark mud track leading to the soldiers' homes. The wind made unwholesome noises. I sang my Christmas carols.

What a brainwave. All three soldiers chorused back. Voices carry long distances in the night, and being light sleepers, all three were quickly awoken by my plaintive songs. My fame as the tower guard contra-tenor had spread far and wide.

But there was no time to celebrate such mundane glories. We sped back to camp on the back of a Datsun pick-up and lived happily ever after.